ce, outwit a **crocodile**, or play music with ss in **Boots**? Will you find **icicles** hanging ill you make the **wicked fairy** cross? Will n make **bread**, ride a dancing **unicorn**, or ou step through a **wardrobe** into another a **broom**? What will you see through your ass? Will you spot a **sneaky wolf** hiding ure? Will you take a **hot-water bottle** with dance with a **duckling**, kiss a **frog**, follow es on the **trees**, find an **ostrich** to ride, e **a magic wand**? Will you sail the seven a **swan**, or trick an **ogre**? Will you find a stion, or choose to live in a **shoe house**? ou spot a **small cricket**, magically change a **tin soldier**, or defeat the **evil wizard**?

For the wonderful charity Home-Start that pairs trained
volunteers with young families in need of some help

P.G.

For all those who have shared their battered You Choose books with me

N.S.

PUFFIN BOOKS

UK | USA | Canada | Ireland | Australia | India | New Zealand | South Africa

Puffin Books is part of the Penguin Random House group of companies
whose addresses can be found at global.penguinrandomhouse.com.

www.penguin.co.uk   www.puffin.co.uk   www.ladybird.co.uk

Penguin
Random House
UK

First published 2020
001

Text copyright © Pippa Goodhart, 2020
Illustrations copyright © Nick Sharratt, 2020
The moral right of the author and illustrator has been asserted

Printed in China
A CIP catalogue record for this book is available from the British Library

ISBN: 978–0–141–37897–8

All correspondence to:
Puffin Books, Penguin Random House Children's
One Embassy Gardens, New Union Square
5 Nine Elms Lane, London SW8 5DA

YOU
CHOOSE
FAIRY TALES

Nick Sharratt & Pippa Goodhart

PUFFIN

Welcome to your fairy tale in a land far, far away.

What kind of hero will you choose to be today?

Which of these fairy-tale homes would suit you?

A castle? A cottage?
A very big shoe?

What will you be good at in this story we are making?

Running? Dancing? Sword-fighting? Or baking?

Every story hero needs at least one loyal friend.

Choose your true companions to be with you to the end.

You're off on an adventure!
The signposts point the way.

Take a road to somewhere new.
Where will you go today?

How will you travel to where you want to go?

Time to stop and have some lunch. What will you choose to eat?

What items might be handy as you go about your quest?

Be prepared – your fairy tale may put you to the test!

Stop! There's danger up ahead – including giant feet!

Which of these baddies would you least like to meet?

What might happen next? There's so much you could do!

Will there be magic or mischief? The choice is up to you!

There's a ball at the palace!
The band will sing and play.

Who will you choose to boogie with as you dance the night away?

Choose a bedtime story,
or make one up instead . . .

Did you make it through that **maze**? Or d
you extinguish a **fiery dragon**, swim with
best friend, or go to the **witch hat towe**
you have a **sword fight,** find **four and**
dormouse in a **teapot,** or ride in a stretc
of **angry sisters?** Did you find the **house**
lion, or drink from the **bottle** that said
fiendish moustache to wear, or watch yo
the **scowly slithery snake?** Did you choose
a **small deer peeping,** or tightrope walk o
house, ride in a **pumpkin coach,** pick fr
wearing a **'G'?** Did you run as fast as a **gi**
give **Tom Thumb** a ride in your pocket, o
the **terrible troll?** Did you live in a h
shoemaker elves flying? Or a **frog eating**
Did you build a **little brick house** with a